Designed by Andrea Newton
Language consultant: Betty Root

This is a Parragon Publishing book
This edition published in 2003
Parragon Publishing, Queen Street House, 4 Queen Street,
BATH BA1 1HE, UK
Copyright © Parragon 2001

ISBN 1-84250-577-7
Printed in Singapore

My Mom is Great

Written by Gaby Goldsack

Illustrated by Sara Walker

p

My Mom is great.
She's so good at everything.
I think my mom's ... MAGIC!

Every morning, her magic begins when she disappears into the bathroom. She changes from morning Mommy ...

into daytime Mommy!

After that, Mom is ready to tackle anything—
even the horrible monsters that
live under my bed.

Isn't my mom brave?

My mom's not afraid of anything.

I'm never worried when she's around.

My mom never lets me down.

She even manages to find Little Ted after I've looked everywhere—and given up hope of ever seeing him again.

Then, for her next trick,
Mom fixes my Mr. Wobbly.

You would never know he'd been broken.

In fact, my mom knows how to fix just about anything ...

except washing machines.

My mom always knows when
I've done something wrong.

But she never stays angry
with me for long.

Mom and I always have fun. Sometimes she takes me for bike rides in the country.

WHEEEEEEEE!

My mom is amazingly smart.

She always knows the answers
to my questions.

And she's a **fantastic** cook.
She makes me the yummiest meals.

TA-DAAAAAA!

My mom makes me smile when I'm sad.

And she can always make me feel better
with a **magical** hug.

Toward the end of the day Mom's magic starts to fade. By the time I'm ready for bed she has changed back into morning Mommy.

But I don't care what Mom looks like. I don't even care if she's not really magic, because whatever she does, she's my mom and ...

my mom is GREAT!